NELLY THE MONSTER SITTER

THE HOTT HEDS AT NO. 87

KES GRAY

ILLUSTRATED BY CHRIS JEVONS

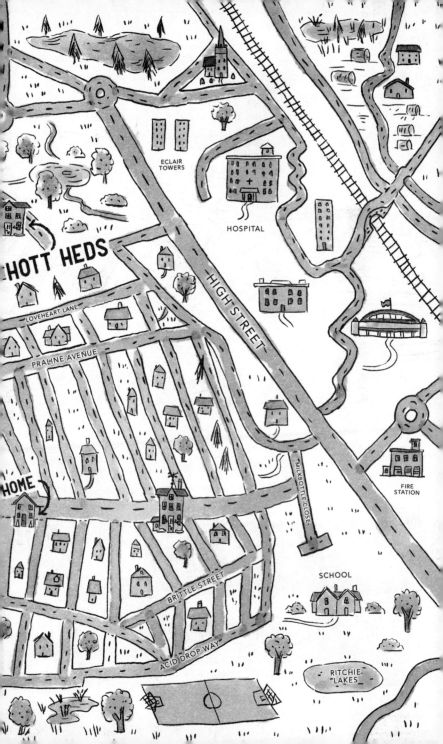

CHAPTER 1

Hallelujah, lo and behold, Nelly's mum and dad had bought a new car! Well, not a *new* new car, but definitely a car that was a whole lot newer than their old Maestro.

'Da dah!' said her dad, climbing out of the driver's seat and polishing the bonnet with the sleeve of his coat. 'Your chariot awaits!'

Nelly looked at the shiny green Volkswagen parked on their drive and smiled. She had a monster sitting appointment that afternoon and for the first time in a very long time she

wouldn't have to persuade her dad to give her a lift!

'It's got a sun roof, leather seats and wait for it … a coffee cup holder!' boasted her dad, crossing the driveway to remove a piece of fluff from the front bumper.

'It isn't red though, is it?' frowned Nelly's twin sister Asti. 'AND it hasn't got a Lamborghini badge on the bonnet. I told you to get a Lamborghini!!!'

'What else has it got?' asked Nelly, ignoring her sister and keeping her dad firmly on track for that lift.

'It has bluetooth, air con, electric windows, a one point five litre engine and wait for it … SATNAV too!' said Mum, stepping out of the front door with all the technical information needed plus two mugs of celebratory coffee.

'Yes, that too,' said her dad, blowing steam from his mug into the chilly November air.

Nelly's spirits soared. 'SATNAV!' she gasped. 'You mean I could get a phone call from a monster family living absolutely anywhere in the country and as long as they know their post code I can baby sit for them without us getting lost on the way?'

'Absolutely!' said her mum.

'I never get lost,' frowned her dad.

In fairness, Nelly's dad never actually had got lost driving Nelly to one of her many monster sitting adventures. In truth though that might have been because all of Nelly's adventures to date had been located on the Montelimar Estate. Familiar territory if you live on … well, the Montelimar Estate.

'You got lost driving to Devon,' said Asti.

'That's because I thought Devon was in Cornwall,' explained her dad.

'And you got lost when we went to Auntie Mabel's funeral,' said Mum.

'That's because the road signs were confusing,' said her dad, 'plus I'd left my black tie at home. You try going the right way to a funeral when you've left your black tie on the back of a sofa.'

'You were the only man at the funeral that wasn't wearing a tie, weren't you, Dad?' said Asti.

'Mum tried to origami you one out of a black paper napkin, didn't she!' laughed Nelly.

'Except it didn't look like a funeral tie at all,' said Asti. 'It looked like a paper aeroplane!'

Nelly looked at her dad. Conversations often went this way in the Morton family household. Dad on a high ... ending with Dad on a low.

'Never mind,' she said, keen to put some instant wind back in his sails, 'you won't get lost if you take me monster sitting this afternoon, the Hott Heds only live in Truffle Lane!'

Asti's eyes bulged.

'THE WHAT HEADS?!!' she choked.
'What kind of repulsive, revolting creatures are you baby sitting for now??!!!!!'

'The Hott Heds at number 87,' said Nelly. 'And he's not a baby, he's seven.'

'They actually sound rather fun!' smiled her mum.

'Fun?!' gasped Asti. 'How can you possibly be fun if you've got nine heads, bad breath, tentacles, hairy eyeballs, green teeth, dribble all over your face and slimy fingernails?'

Nelly's eyebrows arched skywards.

'Slimy fingernails!?' she exclaimed. 'Where did you get slimy fingernails from!?' Even Nelly hadn't encountered those before.

'I didn't mean slimy fingernails,' Asti faltered. 'I meant fingernails that don't have any nail varnish on them!'

Nelly placed her hands on her hips and glared.

'Not everyone has nail varnish on their brain. Or nail varnish FOR a brain!' she fumed.

Mum stepped in before the sister wars had a chance to escalate.

'No more of this both of you, PLEASE!' she insisted. 'If your dad and I have heard this monster nonsense once, we have heard it a trillion times. Never mind what either of you think about monsters or nail varnish! We have a new car. It has bluetooth, air con, electric windows, a hybrid engine, satnav …'

'And a coffee cup holder!' beamed Dad.

'Shall we try it out?' said Nelly, seizing the

opportunity to be the first sibling to sit in the passenger seat.

'Excellent idea!' said her dad, draining the last slurp from his mug. 'Then maybe you could find me a postcode for Truffle Lane.'

'But you know the way to Truffle Lane, Dad,' said Nelly, opening the passenger door. 'We've driven down there loads of times before on the way to the park.'

'I know,' said her dad with a wink. 'I'm just interested to see if the satnav knows the right way too!'

CHAPTER

The coffee cup turned out to be a bit of a squeeze. Its base could just about be wedged into the cup holder but the handle on the mug scuppered any chances of it squeezing in further.

'I think it's meant for coffee shop type cups,' said Nelly. 'Or water type bottles.'

Nelly's dad sighed, eased back into the driver's seat and practised putting on his new seat belt.

'Start her up then,' said Nelly, clicking her

own seat belt. 'You can take me for a spin!'

'I thought you'd never ask,' smiled her dad, pressing the ignition button and dropping the car into reverse gear.

'Don't go without MEEEE!' screeched Asti, abandoning her mum on the doorstep and banging on the bonnet of the car.

Nelly's face fell at the prospect of sharing a confined space with her sister; any space with her sister actually. Asti was such a pain.

'Actually, Dad,' sighed Nelly, unclipping her seat belt, 'I need to get ready for my visit to the Hott Heds. Let Asti have the first test ride.'

Nelly's dad waited patiently for the two sisters to swap places. 'Don't forget to find me that postcode,' he called.

Nelly nodded, shoved her way past her sister and stomped in the direction of the front door.

'I won't,' she replied from the doorstep. 'And don't forget I need to be at the Hott Heds by half past two!'

With a wave and a toot, the shiny green Volkswagen reversed into Sweet Street. With a wave and a single coffee mug, Nelly and her mum returned indoors.

CHAPTER 3

Autumn was definitely on its way out.

'I love it when you put the central heating on,' said Nelly, stepping back into the hallway. 'The house feels so snug and warm inside.'

'Me too,' said her mum. 'It's a bit early in the year to be turning it on, but hey – if we can afford a new car, what's another couple of pounds on the heating bill!'

'Postcode,' remembered Nelly. 'I need to find Dad his postcode.'

Nelly and her mum parted at the doorway

to the lounge, Mum in the direction of the
dishwasher, Nelly in the direction of the family
computer.

Unsure whether monsters actually knew about postcodes, Nelly had decided not to risk embarrassing the Hott Heds by asking them direct.

Google, she was sure, would have the answer.

And she was right.

OC6 1ZB was the postcode for Truffle Lane. Whether or not satnav would be able to compete with dadnav on the 'getting there' front would remain to be seen.

With the Hott Heds' postcode tattooed in biro on the back of her hand, Nelly left the lounge and headed for her bedroom.

'I must check my notebook for special requests,' she reminded herself as she jogged up the stairs.

Monster families often asked Nelly in advance to bring something to a monster sitting visit, especially if there were a few surprises in store. If there *had* been a special request from the Hott Heds, then Nelly knew exactly where to find it.

'Let's have a looksy,' she whispered, skipping into her bedroom and opening her bedside drawer.

Every special request that a monster had ever made of Nelly was recorded in the pages of her monster-sitting notebook. She had once been asked to take a suitcase full of clothes to the Thermitts, she had twice been asked to wear roller blades to the Dompledores,

the Manixes had asked her
to wear camouflage
netting,

and the Waknutters had asked her take an egg
whisk, a bucket of ping pong balls and a pair of
rubber gloves.

That
was a very
long story.

Intrigued and a little bit excited, Nelly sat down on her bed and lifted her notebook from the drawer. With some expert flicks of the pages she homed in on *Saturday 29th November 14.30–16.30 p.m.*

'SHOE SIZE?!' she frowned. The Hott Heds had asked her for her shoe size!

She remembered telling them over the phone that she was a size four, but why they wanted to know she really had no idea.

She looked down at the shoes she was wearing, the ones she was always wearing. They were her favourite Converse style trainers, fourteen lace holes, red fabric, white soles. She had worn them to every monster sitting adventure she had ever been on and this afternoon would be no exception.

By 13.30 she had dressed in her green jeans and sardine sweatshirt, written the Hott Heds' address on a post-it and slapped it on the hallway mirror. All she needed now was a shiny green Volkswagen to transport her.

87
TRUFFLE
LANE

'Mummmm!!! When do you think Dad and Asti will be back?' she shouted, opening the front door to find the driveway as empty as she had left it. 'They've been ages!'

'He's gone to Gym Kingdom!' her mum shouted back from the kitchen.

'What's he gone there for?' shouted Nelly.

'To buy a water bottle, apparently!' replied Nelly's mum. He might be a while!'

CHAPTER 4

Thumb twiddling wasn't something that Nelly was particularly good at doing. She was a doer, not a twiddler. By the time her dad had reappeared on the driveway, she hadn't just transferred the Hott Heds' postcode to her monster-sitting notebook, she had transformed it into a work of art.

'You were right, Nelly!' her dad chimed from the open car window. 'A water bottle fits perfectly into my cup holder! So does my takeaway medium cappuccino!'

Nelly gave her dad a double thumbs-up from the doorstep. It was becoming increasingly apparent that he had bought himself a coffee cup holder with a car attached.

'My large hot chocolate with extra cocoa powder and marshmallows fits perfectly too!' gloated Asti, climbing out of the car and raising her takeaway cup like an Olympic torchbearer. 'YUM!'

Nelly frowned. A spin round the block had become a spin round the block, a trip to Gym Kingdom and a stop off at the Coffee Library too.

More importantly, her sister had been treated and wasn't about to share.

'Take the marshmallows back to your bedroom,' Nelly scowled. 'They can be your new best friends.'

There was nowhere further Nelly could go with this one, short of slapping the large hot chocolate with extra marshmallows out of Asti's hand or pouring it over her head.

Positive thoughts were her only way
forward.

'I got the postcode, Dad!' she shouted,
raising her right arm and pointing the back of
her hand at him. 'OC6 1ZB!'

Nelly's dad's head and elbow disappeared
back inside the car instantaneously.

'DONE!' he replied, reappearing with a
thumbs-up of his own.

'OK,' smiled Nelly, scowling at her sister.
It was five to two and pretty much time to go.
With a wave to her mum, Nelly headed for her
lift.

'I wonder if the Hott Heds have got a cup
holder in their car?' said her dad, as Nelly
climbed into her seat.

'I doubt very much they have a car, Dad,' said Nelly, with a tug of her seat belt. 'Monsters don't go out unless they can get a baby sitter, remember?'

'Of course,' nodded her dad, reversing the car off the drive. 'You've been monster sitting for so long now, sometimes I forget how lucky these monsters are to have found you.'

'I'm the lucky one,' said Nelly. 'If I didn't go monster sitting, I'd be stuck indoors with Asti.'

Nelly's dad refused to be drawn on that topic, choosing instead to think satnav.

'*Route guidance will commence now,*' it purred.

CHAPTER
5

'So far so good!' smiled Nelly's dad.

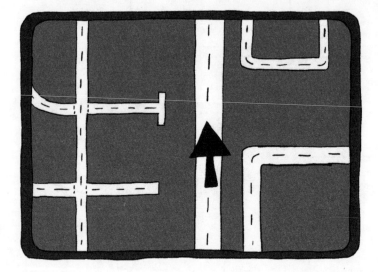

'*Continue on the current road for four hundred metres,*' said the satnav.

'Correct!' said Nelly's dad, pointing at the screen. 'It says we'll be there in four minutes!'

'*Next left,*' said the satnav.

'Goodness me, she's good. I bet she tells me to take the next right into the High Street though,' said her dad, bracing himself for a glaring satnav error. 'These things always take you along the major roads; no local knowledge, you see.'

'*At the end of the road turn left into Caramel Way,*' said the satnav.

'I stand corrected!' said Nelly's dad, giving his steering wheel a fist bump.

'*Continue on the current road, then take the next left,*' said the satnav, '*and then first right into Truffle Lane.*'

'Well I'll be blowed!' said Nelly's dad. 'Hats off to Delilah! That's what I've decided to call her!'

'Delilah!?' said Nelly. 'You can't call a satnav Delilah!'

'Of course I can,' said her dad, swinging the Volkswagen right into Truffle Lane. 'She sounds every bit like a Delilah to me.'

'*You have reached your destination,*' said Delilah.

Nelly's dad slowed the car to a snail's pace and peered left and right.

'Oh noooooooo,' he sighed. 'This isn't number 87, it's number 4! Delilah, Delilah,

Delilah, right at the very last minute you've let us down!'

Nelly peered out of the window and shook her head.

'We didn't give the satnav—'

'*Delilah*, Nelly,' corrected her dad.

'We didn't give *Delilah* the house number, Dad,' continued Nelly, 'we only gave her the postcode.'

'Then Delilah, you are forgiven!' smiled her dad, blowing a kiss at the satnav screen and then continuing down the lane.

'Here we go, Nelly, here we go,' said her dad. 'We have reached our destinationnnnn nnnnnnnnnnnnnnnnnnnnnnnnnnnNOW!'

he chuckled, pointing at the pavement and then pulling up precisely outside the empty driveway to number 87.

I'd love to live in Truffle Lane, thought Nelly, gazing at the towering tree line that framed each red-brick house. *I bet they get squirrels in their gardens and everything.*

There was no evidence of squirrels in the Hott Heds' front garden. Indeed, there was no evidence of the Hott Heds either. That was generally the way with monster families living secretly on the Montelimar Estate. Unless you happened to ring their doorbell or give their door knocker a rat-a-tat-tat, you would never know they were there. Assuming they answered the door to you in the first place, that is.

Monsters always answered their door to

Nelly the Monster Sitter. Word of Nelly's willingness to baby sit for them had spread like wildfire among the monster community. Monsters on the Montelimar estate were as keen to meet Nelly as Nelly was to meet them.

It was 14.08, she was 22 minutes early, but Nelly's experience of monster sitting had taught her that being early was never a problem.

'Here goes,' she smiled, unclipping her seat belt and climbing out of the car.

'What's our postcode for home, Nelly?' asked her dad, getting ready to punch some new coordinates into the screen.

'You know the way home, Dad,' sighed Nelly.

'I know, but I like talking to Delilah,' said her dad. 'She understands me.'

CHAPTER 6

The driveway of number 87 was tarmacked from top to bottom, long enough for two cars and lined with copper beech hedgerow.

From the pavement there was little or no view of the Hott Heds' front door. A barrier of autumn shrubbery screened the front of the house, leaving the entrance entirely to Nelly's imagination.

It was the front door that Nelly always set her sights on when first visiting a monster's house. Front doors were the key to her every monster sitting adventure.

'Be spotty,' she smiled, adjusting her scrunchy and padding towards the door. 'A spotty front door would be a first!'

Call it a hunch, call it a monster sitter's intuition, but she was almost, definitely certain that it was spotty.

As she approached the end of the hedgerow, her spine began to tingle. Would it be a spotty front door, would it be a spotty front door, would it be a spotty front door …???

. . .

. . .

. . .

. . .

. . .

. . .

It was a red front door; a steel front door, the kind of door she really wasn't expecting.

It had no door knocker.

It had no letter box.

It did have a doorbell, but it was like no doorbell she had ever seen before.

Nelly stood toe to toe with the stone front step and craned her neck forward. The doorbell was located to the right of the door, encased in a red glass-fronted box.

She craned her neck further forward still.

And then further still.

And then further still ...

A message printed on the glass in white type read:

IN CASE OF DOORBELL

BREAK GLASS

Nelly gulped and then gulped again. There was a small hammer hanging from a hook beside the casing: about the length of a biro and forged like an ice pick from heavy-duty steel.

'Surely not,' she murmured. 'Surely the Hott Heds don't really want me to break the glass?'

She took a step back to ponder. Perhaps she should knock on the door instead. Yes, that is exactly what she would do – after all, she couldn't start breaking things the moment she arrived on their doorstep.

Knock, knock went her knuckles on one panel of the Hott Heds' front door.

...

...

Thump, thump went her fist.

…

…

…

Either the Hott Heds weren't in or they
weren't answering.

Nelly took two steps back and craned her
head in the direction of the nearest ground-
floor window. Without pressing her nose to
the glass it was difficult to determine whether
anyone was inside. There were no twitches
from the curtains to suggest her presence had
been noted. There were no noises to be heard
from the other side of the door either.

'Oh well,' she sighed, taking two steps
forward and reaching out with slightly
trembling fingers. 'Break the glass it is!'

The instant Nelly broke the glass on the doorbell, a loud continuous trinnnnnnng erupted from her finger.

She dropped the hammer by her feet and jumped back in a panic. It sounded like a fire alarm, not a doorbell!

'I do hope I haven't set off an alarm!' she gasped.

She hadn't. But she *had* triggered the opening of the Hott Heds' front door.

CHAPTER 7

'Nelly!!!' honked a monster from the doormat. 'How lovely to meet you! My name is Bryant, this is my wife May and this little bright spark here is our son Vesta!'

Nelly's eyes darted to each monster in turn. They had one eye each, no ears that she could see, no eyebrows and no eyelashes either. Their bodies were long, black and stick thin, their heads round and smooth like porcelain light bulbs.

Even more striking, Bryant's head was red, May's head was yellow and Vesta's head was orange!

'They look like matches!' she gasped. 'Matches with arms and legs!'

'Do come in, Nelly, please do come in,' said Bryant, extending a pipe-cleaner-thin arm for a hand shake.

Nelly looked down at the hand she was about to shake.

It was black, with two fingers only, each finger flattened and rounded at each end like the pincers on a pair of traditional fire tongs.

'Pleased to meet you, Bryant,' she answered, returning Bryant's welcome with a firm handshake of her own and then bending with a curtsey to the floor.

'I dropped it by mistake,' she explained, picking the hammer up from the gravel and attempting to return it.

'Sorry about the broken glass, and the noise too,' she added.

The Hott Heds looked at each other and honked uncontrollably.

'We love that noise, don't we, May?' honked Bryant.

'Yes, it's quite our most favourite noise in the world,' agreed May.

Nelly extended the hammer a little further towards them, but the three monsters were having none of it.

'Keep it, Nelly,' May honked. 'You're bound to make use of it later.'

Nelly squeezed the hammer into the front pocket of her jeans, somewhere between her hanky and her mobile phone. *Make use of it later?* she mused. What did the Hott Heds mean by that? She was expecting to make use of her not inconsiderable monster sitting skills, but a hammer? What on earth would she possibly want with a hammer?

'Please, please be our guest,' honked Bryant, ushering her into the hallway with a wave of both arms.

'Thank you, thank you,' replied Nelly, stepping into the house. 'I've been looking forward to meeting you!'

Had Nelly been using her ears as well as she had been using her eyes she would have noticed that the tringing ring of the doorbell had ceased the instant the door had opened. There was no sound in the hallway now. What there was, was the unmistakeable smell of wood smoke.

Nelly sniffed the air as discreetly as she could. The Hott Heds had either been having a bonfire in the garden or they were incredibly bad cooks.

'If you wouldn't mind removing your shoes, Nelly, we'd be very grateful,' honked May. 'We've just had the house re-carpeted.'

Nelly's eyes dropped to her feet. A red shag pile carpet stretched the length and breadth of the Hott Heds' hallway.

'Of course, of course,' she said, parking her bottom on the floor and setting about untying her laces.

'Red's our favourite colour in the world,' smiled Vesta. 'Isn't it, Mumma, isn't it, Dadda?'

Red certainly was the Hott Heds' favourite colour in the world. The carpet in the hall was red, the wallpaper in the hallway was red, the ceiling was red, even the bannister leading up the stairs was painted red.

What's more, after ten seconds of sitting on the carpet, Nelly's bottom was turning red.

'How do you like our under-floor heating, Nelly?' honked May proudly.

'It's very ... hot!' said Nelly, wriggling a little uncomfortably as she prised each trainer off in turn.

'Hot is our favourite temperature,' honked Vesta. 'Isn't it, Mumma, isn't it, Dadda!'

'It certainly is,' Bryant and May nodded. 'Hot is our favourite temperature in the world!'

Nelly stood up gingerly and transferred the heat from her bottom to the soles of her feet. In just a matter of seconds though, her toes began roasting.

Unable to disguise her discomfort, she tried marching on the spot.

'Would you like some slippers, Nelly?' asked Bryant, pointing at the wall directly behind her. 'We guessed you might need some slippers!'

Nelly turned full circle and gasped.

A pair of size four quilted slippers were encased in another glass-fronted red box.

The message on the glass this time read:

'I made them for you myself,' honked May proudly.

'Out of recycled oven gloves!' honked Bryant.

'Break the glass, Nelly!' honked Vesta excitedly. 'Break the glass with your hammer!'

'Here we go again,' Nelly gulped.

The instant Nelly triggered the alarm bell again, the Hott Heds linked arms and began dancing round in circles.

'OH, WE DO SO LOVE THAT

SOUND,' honked Bryant, switching left and then right with May and then skipping country-dancing fashion in the direction of Vesta.

'JOIN IN, NELLY! JOIN IN!' honked Vesta, beckoning Nelly forward with a wave.

'THIS IS QUITE OUR FAVOURITE TUNE TO DANCE TO IN THE WORLD!'

TRIIIIIIIINNNNNNNNNNNNNNNNN NNNNNNNNNNNNNNGGGGGGGGG GGGGGGGGGGG!!!!!!! continued the alarm bell as Nelly grabbed the slippers from the case on the wall and duly joined in the fun.

The Hott Heds' home-made slippers worked a treat, thick enough to keep the under-floor heating at a bearable temperature but light enough to allow Nelly to skip the full length of the hallway and back.

And back.

And back

and back

and back and back

and back and back.

'When will the alarm bell, sorry music, stop ringing, I mean playing?' gasped Nelly, running out of puff, not to mention dance moves.

'As soon as one of us clicks our fingers,' said
Vesta. 'See!'

Nelly pulled up short beside the front door and placed her hands on her knees. With a click of the fingers – or rather *tongers* – on his right hand, Vesta had indeed brought the **TRIIIIIIIINNNNNNNNNNNNNNNNNNNNNNNNNNN NNNNGGGGGGGGGGGGGGGGGGGGGGGG!!!!!!!!** to a stop.

'How do you do that?' panted Nelly, fanning her face with her hand.

'I just do,' honked Vesta with a shrug. 'We all just do.'

Nelly puffed out her cheeks and gave the Hott Heds the most gung-ho smile she could.

She was already out of puff and she hadn't even reached the lounge!

'Let's go through,' honked May. 'We can put our feet up in there!'

'Is there under-floor heating in the lounge too?' asked Nelly, flapping the neckline of her sweat shirt.

'Of course,' honked Bryant. 'What a silly question. Under-floor heating is our favourite type of heating, Nelly.'

'In the world!' added Vesta.

Red, steel-plated and complete with a push-to-open bar, the door to the Hott Heds' lounge was every bit as unusual as the door to the front of their house.

Nelly had seen something similar in a cinema before and at the swimming baths, but

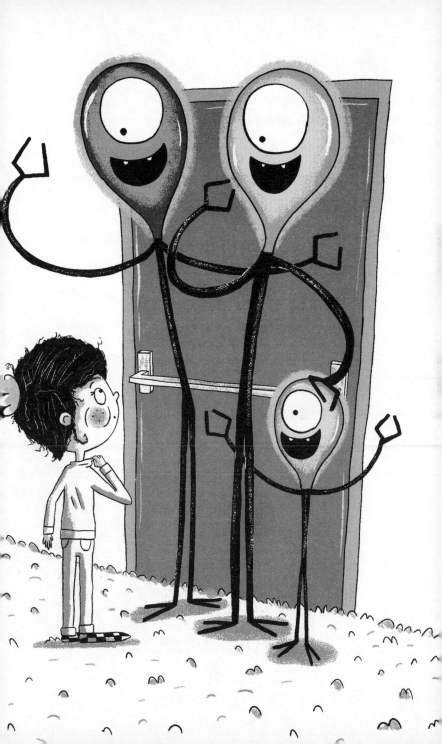

never in a home.

'It's a fire door!' she marvelled, stealing a glance back up the hallway to the one door she had already passed through. 'All of the doors in a Hott Hed house are fire doors!'

'After you, Nelly,' honked Bryant, pushing the metal bar firmly with both hands and then stepping politely to one side.

CHAPTER 8

Nelly sidled into the Hott Heds' lounge, stood, stared, sniffed, sniffed, sniffed and stared again. The smell of wood smoke that she had detected in the hallway hadn't been coming from the kitchen or the garden at all. It was coming from a three-metre-high red air freshener standing Stonehenge-fashion in the centre of the room. Or to be more precise, standing on a red rug in the middle of a red carpet in the centre of the room.

'Wow!' Nelly gasped. 'I've never seen an air freshener that big. The ones we use at home are only about ten centimetres high!'

'This one is three hundred and ten centimetres high, Nelly,' honked May proudly. 'Don't you just adore the smell? It's called Timber Inferno.'

'Timber Inferno is our most favourite fragrance in the world,' honked Bryant.

'In the universe!' honked Vesta. 'I've got one in my bedroom too!'

'We all have,' honked Bryant. 'Couldn't sleep without one.'

Nelly gave her hosts a bewildered grin and then took time out from the air freshener to widen her view of the room. It was difficult to know where to stare first.

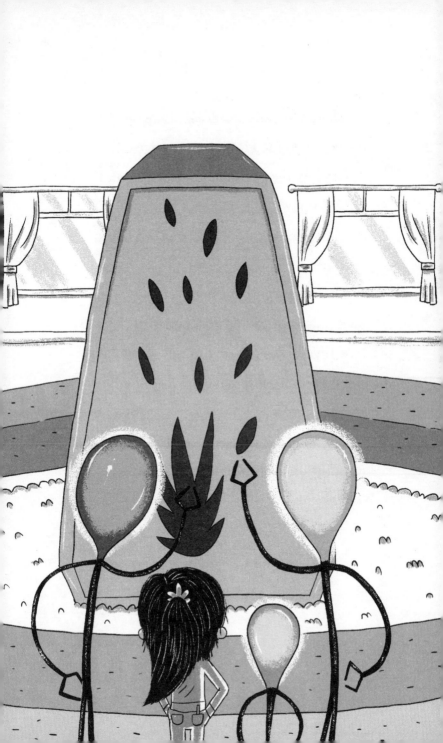

There was a distinct look of fire pit about the centre of the Hott Heds' lounge.

Circling the giant red air freshener and the red rug was a continuous bank of low-level seating, upholstered in red fabric of course.

The red theme continued on the walls, papered red and adorned with expensive-looking red paintings of anything and everything that was, well … red … and hot.

'No watercolours then?' smiled Nelly, admiring an oil painting of an erupting volcano.

'OOOH
NOOOOO!!'

honked the Hott Heds. 'Watercolours are our least favourite paintings in the world.'

Nelly was beginning to understand why.

Heat was definitely the Hott Heds' thing. The fiery red curtains in the front window were perhaps more scarlet than red.

At first, second and third glance every detail of the Hott Heds' lounge appeared carefully chosen ... perhaps with one exception. Assembled along one wall, in a higgledy-piggledy line, six red fire buckets filled with water stood motionless but ready to go.

Maybe it's a contemporary art installation? pondered Nelly.

Whatever it was, it was definitely six fire buckets.

'Please take a seat, Nelly,' honked Bryant, pointing to the centre of the carpet. 'You must be worn out after all that dancing.'

Nelly's eyes turned away from the fire buckets and settled on the circular seat instead.

'Loving the fabric!' she purred, running her palm along the silky-smooth sheen of the seat.

'We do too,' honked Bryant. 'The colour is called "red".'

'Is it really!' smiled Nelly. 'It's very … well, unusual.'

Bryant, May and Vesta sidled their spindly bottoms along the seat, closer to Nelly.

'Now then, the famous Miss Nelly the Monster Sitter,' honked Bryant, 'before May and I leave you and Vesta to play, we want you to tell us all about you!'

'Yes, tell us everything about you, Nelly!' honked Vesta.

Nelly's face flushed red, not so much because of the under-floor heating, more from genuine embarrassment.

She'd been called Nelly before, she'd been called Nelly the Monster Sitter before, but never before 'famous'!

'I'm not sure there is very much to tell really,' she said modestly.

She crossed her legs chat-show fashion and racked her brains for something famous to say.

'Errr ... I'm twelve years old ... I have a twin sister called Asti—'

'WHO?' asked Vesta, his orange head bursting into flames.

Nelly stiffened like a board.

The monster she would shortly be baby sitting was now, to her utter disbelief, on fire, just two monsters' bottoms away from where she was seated!

What's more, no one apart from her appeared to be the slightest bit concerned!!

'Sorry, Nelly,' honked Bryant, reaching calmly for a fire bucket. 'We forgot to tell you ...'

'Vesta has *who fever*,' honked May.

Nelly unstiffened, just enough to gulp.

'Thank you, darling,' May honked, receiving the bucket of water from her husband and carefully pouring it over Vesta's head.

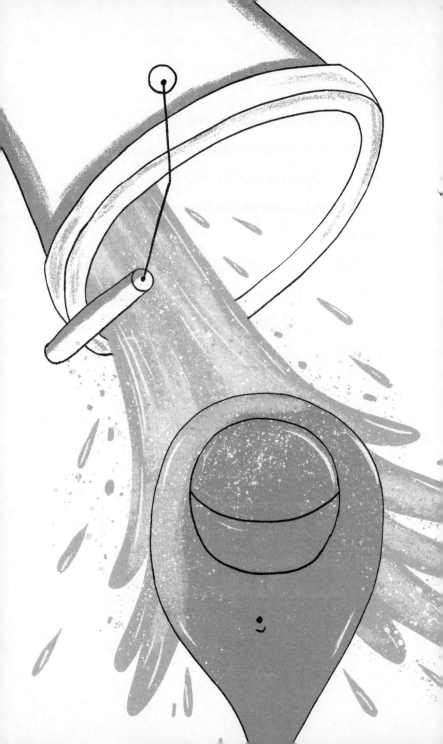

Vesta closed his mouth and shut his eye as the flames went out and a cloud of steam billowed from his shoulders.

'Thanks, Mumma,' he honked. 'Thanks, Dadda.'

Nelly sat goggle-eyed, her mouth open and her mind racing.

'Don't you mean *hay fever*?' she squeaked.

'No, *who fever*,' honked Bryant. 'Please don't mention people that Vesta hasn't heard of ...'

'Or his head will burst into flames,' honked May.

If Nelly's mind had been racing before, it was galloping like a racehorse now. The Hott Heds didn't just look like matches on legs, they WERE matches on legs! And one of them had WHO FEVER! Who did Vesta know and who didn't he know? Who had Vesta heard of and who hadn't he heard of? And who – she meant HOW – was she to know?!

'Now then, Nelly,' honked Bryant, crossing his legs Nelly-fashion, 'carry on, carry on! You were telling us allllllllll about you!

CHAPTER 9

Nelly sat quietly in the red circle and crossed her legs the other way. Then the other way, then the other and the other.

In the light of the information she had just received about Vesta, she was finding her legs a lot easier to move than her mouth.

'I'm twelve years old …' she repeated. 'I …………… …………'

'Have a twin sister called Asti,' honked May. 'It's all right, Nelly, Vesta knows about Asti now because you've just mentioned her, it's perfectly safe to talk about your sister!'

Nelly relaxed a tad, but sighed inwardly. Of all the subjects she could be drawn on, Asti was probably her least favourite in the world.

Could she mention her dad, could she mention her mum? Could she mention Snowball, her rabbit? Or any of her friends at school? If Vesta had burst into flames at the mention of Asti, then he was bound to burst into flames at the mention of them too.

'I live in a house ...' she stammered.

'in a road ...

a bit like this road ...

but not as nice. With ......'

'With what?' honked Bryant.

'Yes, with what?' honked Vesta.

'With.................................

a front door............

painted red ...' continued Nelly, super-cautiously ... 'with a number 111 on it,' she faltered.

'Red like ours???' honked Bryant.

'Yes, red like ours???' honked Vesta, his head still steaming slightly from the fire-bucket incident.

'Annnnnnnnnnnnnnnd ...' stalled Nelly.

The Hott Heds were hanging on her every word.

'Annnnnnnnnnnnnnnnnnnnnnnnnnnnnn nnnnnnnd ....

I've been monster sitting for over a year now!' she said, suddenly gaining inspiration and rattling off a completely fire-proof sentence all in one go!

'Anyone we know?' honked May.

Nelly's shoulders slumped. Now she was in trouble.

Or was she?

'Who do you know?' she probed.

'EVERYONE!' honked May. 'We monsters are a very tightly knit community, you know!'

Nelly breathed a sigh of relief. If the Hott Heds knew EVERY monster living on the estate then every monster she had monster sat for would be known to Vesta!

'Well,' she said, uncrossing her legs, leaning forward and returning to her normal animated self. 'I've baby sat for the Cowcumbers at number 11 …'

'Teet and Bello,' honked Bryant, 'yes, we know Teet and Bello.'

'The Grerks at number 55 ...' continued Nelly.

'I didn't know Scroot and Pummice had children?' honked May.

'I looked after Gluggy, their gog!' said Nelly.

'I want a gog,' honked Vesta.

'They're very licky,' laughed Nelly.

'Too licky,' frowned Bryant. 'Especially for a Hott Hed.'

'Let me think, who else have I monster sat for?' pondered Nelly. 'The Thermitts at number 27 ...'

'Ig and Loo,' nodded May.

'The Water Greeps on the canal ...' continued Nelly.

'Drip and Drop!' confirmed May. 'Lovely monsters, Drip and Drop.'

'I've also monster sat for the Huffaluks, the Muggots, the Wattwatts, the Rimes, the Dendrilegs ...'

'Goodness me!' honked Bryant, walking to the window. 'You have been busy!'

'It really is so kind of you to help us monsters get out of the house for the first time,' honked May.

Nelly waved away the compliment and then looked at her watch. It was already gone three o'clock! Her dad would be coming to pick her up in an hour and a half!

'Talking of getting out of the house for the first time,' she smiled, 'shouldn't you be off? And where exactly are the two of you thinking of going?'

'Ahaaa!!' honked May and Bryant in unison.

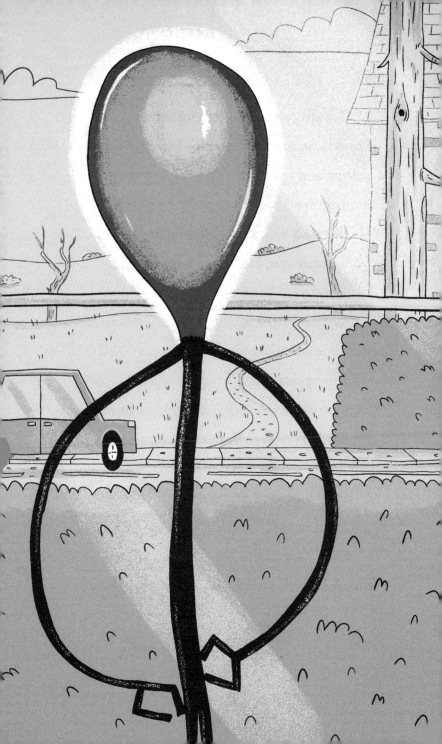

'We are going to solve a mystery!' honked Bryant, swinging his legs over the seating and striding to the window of the lounge.

'We are going to solve a mystery that has been puzzling us for years,' honked May.

'And years,' honked Vesta.

'What mystery is that?' asked Nelly, more than a little intrigued.

'The mystery of the fire in the sky!' honked Bryant, raising his arm high above his head and pointing past the curtains to the heavens.

Nelly turned to May for a little more explanation.

'Every year, Nelly, for as long as we can remember, the sky catches fire, at exactly the same time on exactly the same evening.'

'November the fifth,' honked Vesta.

'Not just November the fifth,' honked Bryant, 'sometimes November the third, sometimes November the fourth …'

'And sometimes on November the sixth or seventh,' honked May.

'But always, always, always definitely on November the fifth,' honked Vesta.

A wave of realisation passed across Nelly's face.

'Guy Fawkes Night!' she exclaimed.

'WHO?' honked Vesta, his head bursting into flames.

Nelly clapped her hands to her cheeks and sprang up from her seat. She'd done it again!

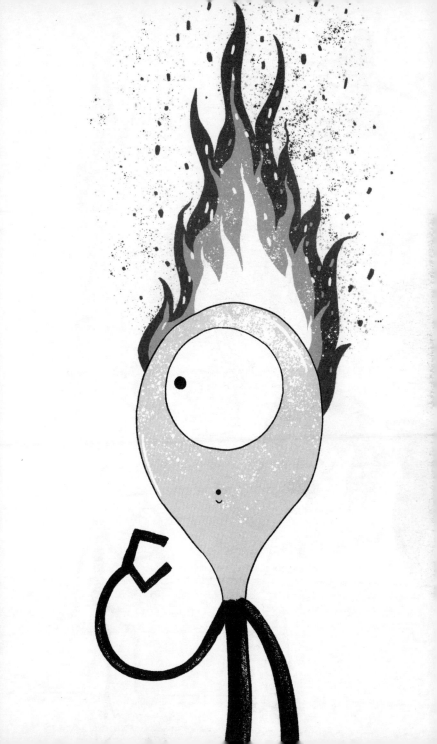

'Guy Fawkes was a gun powder plotter!' she blurted, trying to extinguish the flames with the quickest explanation she could muster. 'He tried to blow up King James the first …'

'WHO?' honked Vesta, the flames on his head leaping a further metre higher still!

'The King of England!' squealed Nelly, 'King James was the King of England in 1605!'

Nelly's lips were moving so fast it was a wonder they didn't catch fire too.

SSPLOSH! went the contents of another fire bucket, emptied this time by Bryant.

SIZZLE! went the top of Vesta's head as the flames fizzled out then turned to steam.

'Thanks, Dadda,' he honked.

Nelly flopped back down on to the seat. Sitting in the lounge with the Hott Heds was more exhausting than dancing up and down with them in the hallway!

'Doesn't it hurt when you do that, Vesta?' she asked.

'Of course it doesn't hurt!' honked Vesta. 'I'm a Hott Hed!'

'It's a bit inconvenient,' honked May, 'especially if we haven't got a bucket of water handy.'

'He'll grow out of it, won't you, son?' honked Bryant.

'I do hope so, Dadda,' smiled Vesta.

Nelly sat motionless for a few more seconds, transfixed by the plumes of steam rising from Vesta's head and shoulders.

'You are the hottest monsters I've ever met by fire, I mean, by far,' she gulped.

'Of course we are, Nelly, we're Hott Heds!' honked Bryant, returning from the window and rejoining the circle once again. 'Now then, Nelly, you were saying?'

'Was I?' asked Nelly.

After all the kerfuffle with the fire bucket, her mind had completely emptied.

'You were about to tell us about Guy Fawkes Night,' honked May. 'What – may we ask – is Guy Fawkes Night?'

Nelly ran her explanation of Guy Fawkes Night through her head first, just to check for potential trip wires. Confident that Vesta now knew who Guy Fawkes and King James the first were and that she could avoid any further 'WHO' moments, she gave it her best shot.

'Every year since the fifth of November 1605, humans have commemorated the Gunpowder Plot. We call it Guy Fawkes Night … after Guy Fawkes. This year, November the fifth was last Saturday.'

'We know!' honked May. 'We were standing in Vesta's bedroom at the back of the house watching it through the window!'

'We watch it through the window every year!' honked Vesta.

'We certainly do,' honked Bryant, 'but I still don't understand how the sky sets on fire? You should see the colours of the flames!'

'Red, orange, yellow, green!' honked May.

'Blue, silver, gold!' honked Vesta.

'They're not flames,' said Nelly. 'Well, they are a type of flame, I suppose … but their proper name is "fireworks".'

'Fireworks?' honked Bryant. 'Tell us more.'

'Basically,' explained Nelly, 'there are all kinds of different fireworks and they come in all kinds of different colours. It depends what chemicals are inside them when they explode.'

'Explode?' honked May in alarm. '*Explode* sounds a bit dangerous!'

'Fireworks *are* a bit dangerous,' agreed Nelly. 'A lot dangerous, actually, that's why you should never light them yourself. Or play around with them. Or even go back to them after they have been lit.'

'At a fireworks party my favourite thing is standing well back from the bonfire and then BOOM! watching the fireworks explode in the sky!'

'I like the sound of fireworks!' honked Bryant.

'BANG!

WHIZZ!

POP!!

and

OOOHH

and

AAAAHHHHH!' honked
May.

'No, that's the people in the park who come
to watch them,' said Nelly.

'WHO?' asked Vesta, his head bursting into
flames yet again.

Nelly sighed, swung her legs in the direction
of the fire buckets and with a remarkable
degree of composure emptied fire bucket
number three over Vesta's head.

'We see you're getting the hang of this!'
clapped May.

Nelly was indeed getting the hang of this.
She was a clever girl who learned fast.

'Thanks, Nelly,' honked Vesta, as another
cloud of steam evaporated from his head.

'And thank you for telling us about Guy Fawkes Night,' honked Bryant.

Nelly returned the empty fire bucket to its higgledy-piggledy line and smiled. 'You'll see exactly where it happens!' she said. 'Because not only are there fireworks at a Guy Fawkes party, there is a gigantic bonfire too! A huge gigantic bonfire that's so big it burns for days!'

'Reaaaaalllly!' honked Bryant. 'Huge gigantic bonfires are our favourite bonfires in the world!'

'It might still be smoking now!' said Nelly.

'Well we'll certainly be looking out for that bonfire!' honked May.

'I wonder what it smells like?' honked Bryant. 'I hope it smells like Timber Inferno.'

'There's only one way to find out!' Nelly laughed.

CHAPTER

At around twenty past three, after a lot of
to-ing, fro-ing and honking, Bryant and May
finally left their home for the very first time.

'Have fun!' said Nelly, waving from the
doorstep. 'The entrance to the park is about
a hundred metres further down the road on
the right!' she said, swinging her arm like a
compass needle. 'I'll see you again at four-
thirty!'

'Will do!' honked Bryant, slipping his arm
lovingly around May's waist. 'You two have fun

as well – and don't forget that Vesta has *who fever*!'

'I won't!' promised Nelly. After three buckets of water, how could she possibly forget?

She and Vesta continued to wave vigorously from the doorstep until one by one, the yellow and red heads of Bryant and May finally disappeared out of view.

'OK, Vesta, it's monster sitting time!' said Nelly, placing her arm on his shoulder. 'What would you like to do now?'

'Play, Nelly,' he honked, 'let's play!'

Nelly looked around. Her mum and dad had told her never to play with matches. What on earth was she meant to do now?

And despite her heat-resistant slippers, her toes were starting to cook.

'If we play outside my tootsies can cool down a bit, Vesta, plus I can put my trainers back on,' she said. 'There isn't any under-floor heating in your back garden, is there, Vesta? Do you have any shoes you like to wear outdoors?'

Vesta shook his head, looked down and shook his head again.

'Hooves are the only things that Hott Heds have on their feet,' he honked.

'Then hooves it is!' said Nelly, turning round and reaching inside the front door. 'Hooves for you and trainers for me!'

'Bear with me,' Nelly said, prising her laces a little looser before sitting down on the front step to tie them.

'Hurry up, Nelly, hurry up!' honked Vesta

excitably. 'Why are you taking so long?'

'I wish I had hooves sometimes,' Nelly
puffed, removing her foot for some more
readjustments and then finally squeezing both
trainers on. 'OK, Vesta, let's go!'

Vesta wheeled away from the front door and
skipped to the side of the house.

'We can get to the back garden this way,' he honked.

'Is your back door open?' asked Nelly, tossing her slippers into the hallway then preparing to pull the front door shut. 'I don't want us to get locked out!'

'Our back door is always open!' honked Vesta.

'Promise?' said Nelly with a frown.

'I promise!' honked Vesta with a cheeky grin.

The alleyway along the side of number 87 was paved with red paving stones and grouted with red grout. Here and there, on the rose trellis attached to the house wall, a few red rose petals were still clinging to summer, although summer had long gone.

At the end of the Hott Heds' side alleyway a tall wooden side gate beckoned. Glossed red, with a red gate latch, it was everything that Nelly had come to expect.

'I bet the back garden is full of red things too,' she whispered to herself. 'Red flowers, red swing, red sand pit, red climbing frame, red trampoline, red everything!'

'After you,' honked Vesta excitedly, unclicking the latch with his tongers and then swinging the side gate wide open.

Nelly strode forward into the garden with a smile and then stopped dead in her tracks.

There was no red in the back garden, there was no green in the back garden. All there was … was …

'Let's play, Nelly!' honked Vesta, abandoning his manners the instant the gate closed behind him. 'Let's play, let's play, let's play!!!'

But Nelly was still in shock.

Her eyes swung right, her eyes swung left. The Hott Heds' back garden was burnt to a crisp! The trees had turned to charcoal, the fence line was scorched from post to post, the lawn was burnt to a cinder, the soil in the flower beds had turned to ash. Even the pollen inside the flowers had turned to soot.

'What happened!?' she gasped.

'What do you mean what happened?' honked Vesta.

'I mean what happened to your back garden?' pressed Nelly. 'It's all burnt!'

Vesta put his hands on his hips, scanned the garden and then honked. And honked and honked and honked and honked!

'Of course it's all burnt! This is where I play!'

Nelly swallowed drily. She was beginning to feel a little uneasy about the prospect of playing in the back garden with a Hott Hed.

'What exactly do you play, Vesta?' she murmured.

'HOT SCOTCH, OF COURSE!' replied Vesta, with the loudest honk of the day.

Nelly's knees began to weaken and the back of her neck began to prickle.

Was that a Hop with a P or a Hot with a T?

'How do you spell Hopscotch?' she quivered.

'H O T S ...' honked Vesta.

'STOP!' blurted Nelly, raising her hand and calling an immediate halt to proceedings. Whatever HOTscotch was, it wasn't a game that she had any intention of playing! She

needed to think of a different game that was completely flame-free and she needed to think of one fast …

'What about Simon Says?' she suggested.

'WHO?' honked Vesta, bursting into flames.

Nelly shook, shuddered, swooned and swayed, then raced to the Hott Heds' back door.

'Please be open, please be open,' she whimpered.

Vesta was right. The door was unlocked.

Through the kitchen, down the hall and into the lounge Nelly sprinted.

'COMING, VESTA!!' she hollered, bursting
into the back garden, fire bucket number four
in hand.

SPLOSHHH!! went the contents of the fire bucket. SIZZLEFIZZLEFIZZ went the steam as it plumed from the top of his orange head.

'Thanks, Nelly,' Vesta honked.

Nelly breathed a sigh of relief, then jumped. 'WAAHHH!' she squealed, as a solitary flame that had escaped her aim suddenly sprouted from Vesta's left cheek.

'SORRY,' she blurted, turning the fire bucket upside down and slamming it over his head.

It was the only thing she could think of to do!

Nelly placed her hands on her knees and gave herself a minute to get her breath back.

Fifty-three seconds into that minute, Vesta tapped on the bucket.

'It's very dark in here, Nelly,' he honked.

(With more than a hint of an echo.)

CHAPTER

When Nelly removed the fire bucket from Vesta's head, they were no longer standing in the back garden. She had used the bucket as a blindfold to lead him back inside. To the kitchen, to be precise.

Nelly had raced through the kitchen so quickly on her previous visit she had barely noticed anything about the room at all. Apart from it being red. There was much to notice now. The counters were topped with red melamine, the floor tiled with red quartz.

Three red high-backed stools lined the units to her left, an array of cooking appliances lined three of the kitchen walls. There was a red gas cooker, a red electric hob, a red range, a red barbeque, a red griddle, a red grill and a red rotisserie too. What there wasn't, as far as Nelly could see, was a sink or any taps.

'Aren't we going to play hotscotch?' honked Vesta, a little disappointedly.

'No, Vesta, I'm afraid we're not going to play HOTscotch,' said Nelly. 'What other things do you like doing?'

Vesta grinned and pointed to the right-hand wall of the kitchen.

'I like eating,' he honked. 'Eating is one of my most favourite things to do in the world.'

'Goodness,' Nelly gasped. 'What are those?'

'It looks like coal?' she murmured, stepping
forward for a closer look.

'It IS coal!' honked Vesta. 'Yum yum!'

'YUM YUM???' frowned Nelly. Surely the

Hott Heds didn't eat coal?

She moved forward for an even closer inspection. The instructions on the cases suggested otherwise.

IN CASE OF BREAKFAST.
BREAK GLASS.

IN CASE OF LUNCH.
BREAK GLASS.

IN CASE OF SUPPER.
BREAK GLASS.

'Oh my goodness,' Nelly murmured. 'The Hott Heds DO eat coal!'

'Break the glass, Nelly break the glass!' honked Vesta. 'We can have a little dance before we eat!'

Nelly slipped her hand into the front pocket of her jeans. The hammer she had been gifted by the Hott Heds was still there, but should she use it? After all, breaking glass wasn't something she was entirely comfortable doing.

'If I break the glass, which one should I break?' she asked, taking Hott Hed meal times anything but for granted.

'The lunch one, of course,' honked Vesta with a clap of his hands. 'I had supper when I woke up this morning!'

Nelly nibbled her lip.

Vesta continued clapping.

'BREAK THE GLASS! BREAK THE GLASS! BREAK THE GLASS!' he honked.

'Oh well, here goes,' smiled Nelly, pulling the hammer from her pocket and raising it shoulder-high.

TAP! went the hammer.

CRACK! went the glass.

TRINNNNNNNNNNGGGGG!!

went the alarm bell.

'Let's dance, let's dance!' honked Vesta, grabbing Nelly by her free hand and leading her in a circle around the kitchen. 'I love this music, don't you?'

'My feet are sticking to your floor tiles!' shouted Nelly, skipping past the cooker and

back again. 'I think the under-floor heating is melting the soles of my trainers!'

'Oops!' honked Vesta. 'You need to put your slippers back on!'

The two unlikely dance partners do-si-doed through the door of the kitchen and down the hallway in the direction of Nelly's heat-resistant slippers.

'Got 'em!' honked Vesta, scooping them up near the front door and tucking them under

his arm. 'You can put them back on while we are having lunch!' he honked.

Nelly would rather have put them on straight away – her toes were beginning to cook – but Vesta had a lot more dancing to do.

Into the kitchen and then back to the front door they promenaded. Twice more round the kitchen, once round the lounge.

'I really do need to change my shoes, Vesta!' Nelly shouted above the din of the alarm bell. 'Or I won't have any trainers left!'

'OK then,' grinned Vesta. 'Let's go and have some lunch!'

With the click of Vesta's tongers the alarm bell ceased immediately.

'I wish I could do that to my sister,' puffed Nelly wearily. She was all danced out.

'Let's eat, let's eat,' honked Vesta excitedly.

'Slippers on first, remember,' Nelly panted, hopping on alternate feet to the nearest kitchen stool.

Her feet were smoking. The underfloor heating had indeed melted the soles of her trainers and any tread she had arrived with had now well and truly vanished.

'Coal?' asked Vesta politely.

Nelly looked at a rather unappetising

plate of food. While she had been changing

her footwear, Vesta had been preparing
lunch.

'There's three pieces of coal each,' he
honked, raising a lump to his mouth and
biting into it with a crunch.

Nelly shuddered.

'Humans don't eat coal I'm afraid, Vesta,'
she grimaced.

Vesta wiped some coal dust from his mouth
and stared back in disbelief.

'Don't eat coal?' he honked. 'EVERYONE
eats coal!'

'Humans don't,' smiled Nelly. 'We eat nice
things like apples and bananas and yogurt and
sausages instead.'

'Yeurk!' honked Vesta. 'They don't sound
very nice at all!'

'Humans eat lots of different things actually,' said Nelly. 'Lots of different things cooked in lots of different ways.'

'Mumma and Dadda cook coal in lots of different ways too,' honked Vesta, opening a kitchen drawer and pulling out an armful of

monster recipe books. 'They do roast coal, smoked coal, barbecued coal, deep-fried coal, minced coal, braised coal, grilled coal, fried coal, and baked coal too. I prefer it raw.'

'I can see that!' laughed Nelly. 'You're already on your third piece!'

Vesta dabbed his lips again, this time using a napkin from a drawer.

Nelly shuffled the recipe books into readable position and flicked through them.

Ready Steady Coal!, Christmas Coal, Coal in Fifteen, MMMM Coal, One Ingredient.

Goodness me! thought Nelly. *Coal is ALL that Hott Heds eat!*

'Sooooooo Nelly,' Vesta honked, with a lick of his lips. 'If humans don't eat coal, does that mean ...'

'That you can have my three pieces of coal to eat too? Yes, it does.' Nelly smiled, handing him back the cookery books along with her plate.

Vesta's single eye widened with delight. 'You must come monster sitting again!' he honked.

'I'll bring a banana for you to try if I do,' laughed Nelly. 'Or a red-hot chilli pepper!'

Vesta shuddered with disapproval.

Nelly leaned back on her stool and gave the kitchen a full 360 scan.

'Vesta, where are your taps?' she asked. 'I'm guessing you might be needing a drink after eating all that coal. Actually, I wouldn't mind a drink of water myself, it's thirsty work monster sitting for a Hott Hed!'

Vesta swallowed drily and shook his head.

'Hott Heds don't have taps, Nelly,' he honked. 'Or drink water. Hott Heds don't drink at all.'

Nelly blinked slowly and then tried with some difficulty to digest what Vesta had just said.

'Don't drink at all?!' she gulped. 'Everyone needs to drink something!'

'We don't,' honked Vesta. 'Drink makes us damp on the inside.'

Nelly's eyebrows arched. There was a weird kind of logic to what Vesta had just told her, but seriously ... Hott Heds didn't drink AT ALL?

'There's rain water in the fire buckets if you're thirsty,' honked Vesta.

'No thank you,' Nelly shuddered. 'I'm not

that desperate. And anyway, I need the water in the fire buckets for emergencies! I've only got two left!'

With the coal devoured and the broken glass despatched to a red pedal bin with a red dustpan and brush, Nelly set her sights on entertaining Vesta for the rest of her stay.

Remember he has who fever, remember he has who fever, she reminded herself. *Whatever we do, wherever we go, we want absolutely no more 'WHO's!*

'WOULD YOU LIKE TO SEE MY BEDROOM!?' honked Vesta.

'I'd love to see your bedroom!' she smiled.

CHAPTER

12

With every stair that Nelly and Vesta climbed, the smell of Timber Inferno grew stronger.

'How many air fresheners do you have up here?' asked Nelly, her nostrils beginning to twitch.

'Ten,' honked Vesta. 'One in my bedroom, one in Mumma and Dadda's bedroom and eight spare ones in the loft. It's a wonderful fragrance, isn't it?'

'Oh yes,' said Nelly with a cough.

'This is my bedroom,' honked Vesta, as they reached the top of the stairs. 'First room on the right!'

Nelly glanced in the direction of Vesta's outstretched tonger. Another red fire door was approaching.

'Make yourself comfortable, Nelly,' honked

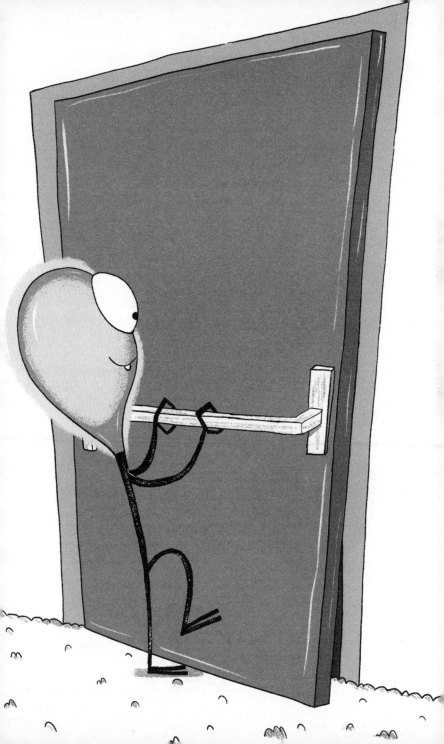

The room that Nelly stepped into was more
of a box room than a bedroom, for the bed
that Vesta slept in wasn't a bed at all. It was a
box. A giant matchbox, for want of a better
description.

'This is how I make my bed, Nelly,' he
honked, sliding the outer casing shut.

'And this is how I get into bed,' he honked,
sliding the hull of the box open, climbing
inside and then lying down with a wave. 'Cosy,
eh?!'

Nelly smiled. She wasn't sure 'cosy' was the right word for it, but 'different' certainly was.

'That really is a very big air freshener,' she said, turning towards the wall at the end of Vesta's bed (box).

'Timber Inferno is the best!' honked Vesta.

'I like your posters too,' she said, looking

round at the pin-ups that adorned Vesta's bedroom walls.

'Those are pictures of my five favourite hot things in the whole wide world,' honked Vesta, pointing to each poster in turn.

'That is my favourite hot thing on Earth, it's called a desert!'

'Yes, I've seen a picture of a desert before,' smiled Nelly.

'Do you know how hot a desert can get?' honked Vesta. '136 degrees! I'd love to go to a desert when I'm older!'

'And what are these posters here?' asked Nelly, more than a little interested.

'Those are my favourite hot things not on

Earth,' honked Vesta. 'This is a planet called Venus,' he pointed.

'Yes, I've heard of Venus before,' nodded Nelly.

'Venus is the hottest planet in the Solar System,' Vesta honked. 'Guess how hot Venus is, Nelly? 860 degrees! I'd love to go to Venus when I'm older.'

'You better start saving for a space rocket!' chuckled Nelly.

'This is my favourite nebula,' honked Vesta, moving on to the next poster and then the next. 'And this is my favourite quasar,' he honked.

'But this one ... this one here is my favouritest, favouritest, favouritest hot, hot, hot thing in the whole wide universe! Can you guess what it is, Nelly?'

'It looks like the sun,' smiled Nelly.

'It IS called the sun, Nelly!' honked Vesta. 'Guess how hot the sun is in the very centre!'

'A million degrees?' guessed Nelly.

'More!' honked Vesta.

'Five million degrees?' guessed Nellly.

'MORE!' honked Vesta.

'Ten million degrees?' frowned Nelly. She was starting to feel a little uneducated.

'TWENTY-SEVEN MILLION DEGREES!' honked Vesta. 'Imagine how hot that is! I would love to go to the centre of the sun when I'm older!'

'I'll let you borrow my slippers if you do!' Nelly laughed.

Nelly's eyes hopped once again to each of the five posters in turn.

'You certainly know a lot about the Solar System, Vesta!' she said.

'Me and my family are always looking at the stars,' honked Vesta. 'That's how we first noticed the fireworks in the park.'

Ah, the park. In all the excitement Nelly had almost forgotten that Bryant and May were having their own adventure in the park.

Nelly perched her bottom on the side of Vesta's bed (box).

'So what time is bedtime for a seven-year-old Hott Hed called Vesta?' asked Nelly.

'Seven o'clock,' honked Vesta. 'When I was six I went to bed at six, when I'm eight I will go to bed at eight, when I'm nine I will go to bed at nine ...'

'I get the idea,' smiled Nelly.

'But I will only ever go to sleep if my Mumma or Dadda has read me a bedtime story first,' Vesta honked. 'Unless I'm really tired.'

'I was the same once!' laughed Nelly.

'You can read me a story now if you like, Nelly!' honked Vesta.

'You won't fall asleep if I do, will you?' laughed Nelly.

'Of course not,' honked Vesta, opening the red door of his red bedside cupboard. 'It's not even my bedtime, plus I'm not even the slightest bit tired. These are my favourite five bedtime stories in the world, Nelly. Choose one!'

Nelly held out her hands and received five red-hot Hott Hed children's book classics.

Nelly marvelled at each and every title. They sounded much more exciting than the non-Hott Hed

OLDILOCKS *and the* THREE DRAGONS

CHARLIE AND THE MOLTEN LAVA FACTORY

mes and the Giant Chilli Pepper

WHO FLAMED ROGER RABBIT?

The Wind in The Bellows

versions she had
grown up with.

'I know a wizard character you'd really enjoy
reading about!' she chuckled, laughing in
advance at her own joke. 'Harry Hotter!'

'WHO?' honked Vesta, his orange head
bursting into flames.

'WAAAAHHHH!' squealed Nelly, hurling
the books to the floor. Not only was Vesta's
head on fire, he had climbed back into his bed

(box) and the headboard of the bed (box) had caught light too!

Nelly flew out of the bedroom and down the stairs in search of fire bucket number five.

How she didn't spill any water on the way back up, she really didn't know.

SPLOSH!

went the contents of the bucket.

SIZZLEFIZZZZZZ

went the steam as it evaporated from Vesta's head (and head board).

'Thanks, Nelly,' honked Vesta, with a smile.

'Can we go back downstairs to the lounge now please, Vesta,' panted Nelly.

'Yes, I think we probably should,' Vesta honked.

CHAPTER 13

Nelly stared ruefully at the higgledy-piggledy line of fire buckets. She only had one full bucket left!

'Are you sure there are no taps in your house, Vesta?' she asked. 'If you had a tap I could refill all six buckets.'

'Sorry, Nelly,' honked Vesta from the circular seat in the lounge. 'Hott Heds don't do taps.'

'What about a shower, or a bath?' she asked, not very hopefully.

'Hott Heds don't have showers,' honked Vesta. 'And we certainly don't have baths! Far too wet!!'

Nelly stared at the last bucket standing and nibbled her lip.

'I'm going to have to be super, super, super careful from now on,' she murmured to herself.

She was tempted not to say another word to Vesta for the entire rest of her visit, but the little Hott Hed put paid to that idea with his very next sentence.

'What are we going to do together now, Nelly?' he honked, patting the red cushion beside him. 'Freeb told me you were full of brilliant ideas!'

Nelly sighed inwardly. Freeb was the only daughter of Blob and Grit, the Huffaluks at number 42. She had monster sat for the Huffaluks on many occasions and if Freeb had been singing her praises, then she was really going to have to up her game.

'I know a game we can play!' said Nelly with a sudden burst of inspiration. 'It's a game I've made up to play with a Hott Hed just like you!'

'Sounds exciting!' honked Vesta, as Nelly joined him on the seat.

'I'm not sure I'd go as far as that,' said Nelly, shuffling her bottom sideways so that she could keep Vesta squarely in her sights. 'But at least I can guarantee you won't burst into flames if we play it!'

'What's the game called?' honked Vesta.

'It doesn't have a name,' said Nelly being super, super, super cautious. 'But this is how we play it. I'm going to think of some things that humans like to eat or drink. The name of each thing will have two or three words in it, but one word will always be missing. What you have to do is guess what the missing word is. Gottit?'

'Gottit!' honked Vesta.

'OK,' said Nelly. 'Here goes. Clue number one … This thing is something that humans enjoy eating at Easter time. It's really tasty, it's got currants in it and it's called a *Something* Cross Bun. What's the missing word?

Vesta crossed his legs, folded his arms, and furrowed his one and only eye and brow.

'Scorching!' he honked.

'Not quite,' said Nelly.

'Warm!' honked Vesta.

'You're getting warmer,' smiled Nelly.

'Baking!!' honked Vesta.

'You're getting warmer still,' sighed Nelly.

'Fiery, sizzling, blazing!!!' honked Vesta.

'Warmer still!' said Nelly.

'Heated!' honked Vesta.

'Like heated only much shorter …' said Nelly, urging him on with some dancing eyebrows of her own. 'Three letters shorter in fact.'

'HOT!' honked Vesta.

'CORRECT!' cheered Nelly with a clap. 'Well done, Vesta, it is indeed a HOT Cross Bun!'

'Ask me another one, ask me another one!' honked Vesta, his eyebrow springing up and down like a flea.

Nelly racked her brains for a moment and then switched back to quizmaster mode.

'OK. Clue number two … This drink that humans like … is really lovely to drink on a day like today or … maybe just before going to bed. It's brown and if you're lucky it will have squirty cream squirted on top of it. Humans call the drink *Something* Chocolate. What's the missing word?'

'Give me another clue,' honked Vesta impatiently.

'OK,' sighed Nelly, realising that Vesta might need a little more help than she'd anticipated. 'Are you listening very carefully, Vesta? I hope you are, because once again, the missing word you are looking for means the opposite of cold.'

'Burning chocolate!' honked Vesta.

'Not burning chocolate, no,' said Nelly with a giggle.

'Boiling chocolate!' honked Vesta.

'No, not boiling chocolate either,' chuckled Nelly.

'Flaming chocolate! Smoking Chocolate! Searing Chocolate! Volcanic chocolate!' honked Vesta, his face turning redder than the lounge.

Nelly slapped her hand to her forehead. Her new game was proving harder for Vesta to play than she'd ever imagined.

'OK, OK, Vesta, I'll give you another clue!' she said. 'The missing word you are looking for is exactly the same word that was missing in the first question.'

'HOT!' honked Vesta.

'CORRECT!' cheered Nelly. 'Very well done, Vesta, it is indeed HOT Chocolate!'

Vesta was on a roll. He'd got two answers right in a row with barely any help from Nelly at all. Well, so he'd convinced himself.

'I think I know how to win at this game now, Nelly!' he honked. 'Give me another clue!'

Nelly was on to a winner too, with a new

game that was fireproof from start to finish!

'Clue number three, Vesta,' she beamed.
'This food is a very popular human food
that actually sounds like an animal! It started
in Germany but they are really popular in
America. It can be a frankfurter or a sausage in
a long bread roll and humans call it a *something*
dog. What's the missing word?'

'HOT DOG!' honked Vesta, beside himself
with excitement.

'CORRECT!' cheered Nelly. At last the
penny had dropped for her little Hott Hed
friend. 'It is indeed a HOT dog!'

'I knew it was, I knew it was!' honked Vesta,
springing to his feet and doing a victory lap
around the lounge. 'Ask me another one, ask
me another one, Nelly. I'm definitely going to

get the next one right too. I just know it!'

Nelly racked her brains for a moment and then smiled. She had decided to stick with the food theme but switch from America to Italy for her inspiration.

'This food—'

'You forgot to say *clue number four*,' interjected Vesta.

'Sorry,' sighed Nelly. 'Clue number four … Ready?'

'I'm ready,' honked Vesta, returning to his seat and concentrating harder than he'd ever concentrated before.

'This food,' continued Nelly. 'This food is … is—'

'If I get this one right it will be four in a row,' interrupted Vesta again.

'Yes, I know,' said Nelly, beginning to lose her thread altogether. 'Now where was I?'

'This food is … is,' honked Vesta.

'Precisely,' nodded Nelly. 'This food … may I continue, Vesta?' she asked.

'Of course, of course,' honked Vesta. 'If you don't continue I won't be able to make it four–nil to me. Please carry on …'

Nelly took a deep breath and went for it.

'Clue number four. This food is loved by humans all over the world too. It is a very flat, very round type of food. It has tomato sauce on it, mozzarella cheese, pepperoni and peppers and is called an American *Something* pizza. What's the missing—'

'HOT!' honked Vesta. 'It's an AMERICAN HOT PIZZA ISN'T IT NELLY!!!'

'Yes, it is an Americ—' Nelly tried to reply.
But Vesta was out of there.

Twice round the garden,

three times round the lounge,

up and down the stairs.

If he had been wearing a football shirt he
would definitely have pulled it over his head.

Nelly giggled and then applauded Vesta roundly. Arms aloft, he had burst back into the lounge and skidded across the carpet on his knees.

'I love games!' he honked. 'Especially new games that I'm really good at!'

'I love new games too,' smiled Nelly. 'I bet you're looking forward to Christmas!'

'I'm REALLY looking forward to Christmas,' honked Vesta. 'I love Christmas, Nelly!' he danced. 'Christmas is my most favourite time of year!'

'Mine too!' Nelly smiled. 'What are you hoping Father Christmas will bring you?'

'WHO?' honked Vesta, bursting into flames.

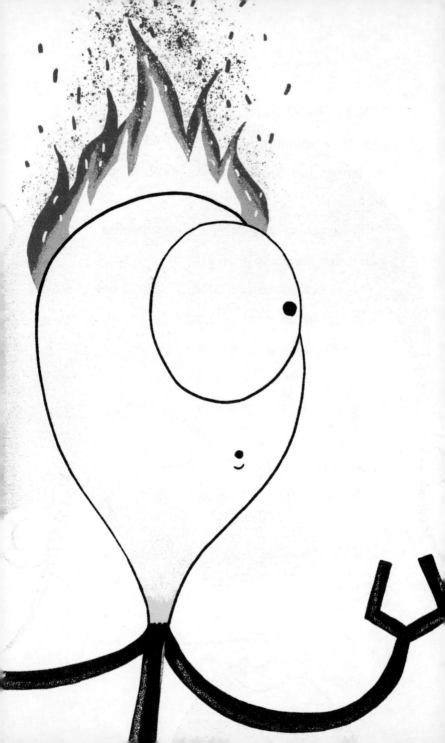

Nelly's eyes widened and her mind went into free fall. Words began to tumble from her mouth like the jackpot from a fruit machine, but in her haste to undo what she'd done, she only made things worse.

'Not Father Christmas!' she blurted.

'WHO?' honked Vesta again.

'I mean Santa *CLAWS*!
... Not Santa *CLAUS*!...'
'WHO?' honked Vesta.

'Santa CLAWS with a W!' Nelly squeaked, racing for the fire bucket. 'Not Santa CLAUS with a U!'

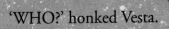

'WHO?' honked Vesta.

'I know that monsters don't believe in Father Christmas or Santa Claus with a U,' gasped Nelly, lunging for the full fire bucket and hurling the contents in the direction of Vesta's head.

SPLOSH went the water.
SIZZLEFIZZLESIZZLE FIZZ
WHOOOOSSSHHHHHH!!! went the steam,
as Vesta's head was briefly extinguished but
then immediately reignited again.

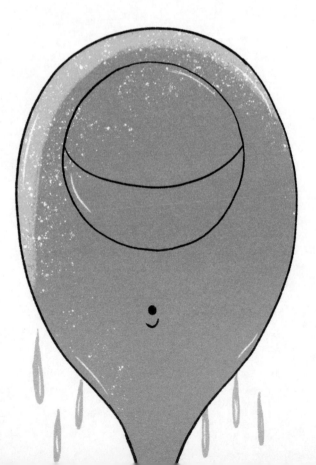

'WHO? WHO?' he honked, the flames on his head pluming like a flame thrower in the direction of the ceiling.

Nelly's lips kept motoring.

'Monsters believe in Santa CLAWS instead, don't you, Vesta!' blurted Nelly, lowering the empty bucket to her side. 'Santa Claws with a W is a great big jolly old centipede with lots and lots of claws and I believe in him too because I saw him come down the chimney last Christmas when I had Christmas Day supper with the Dendrilegs!'

But it was no good. And far too late. With every 'WHO' that Vesta had whoed the flames on his head had blazed higher. His head had set fire to the ceiling, the ceiling had set fire to the walls, the walls had set fire to the paintings, the paintings had set fire to the carpet, the carpet had set fire to the rug, the rug had set fire to the air freshener – even the seat they had been sitting on was starting to smoulder!

The Hott Heds' beautiful lounge was completely ablaze and it was going to take a lot more than six empty fire buckets to extinguish it!

'I'm calling the fire brigade!' she said, grabbing Vesta's hand and wrenching her mobile phone from her pocket.

'WHO?' honked Vesta.

'And the police! And the ambulance service! And the coast guard! And the army! And the navy! And the air force! and anyone else that will come!'

'WHO?WHO?WHO?WHO?WHO?' honked Vesta.

'AND STOP SAYING WHO!' hollered Nelly.

'Thanks, Nelly,' honked Vesta from the front doorstep.

He was feeling a little winded after being propelled across the front lawn by a fire hose.

'Don't mention it,' sighed Nelly, her breath billowing like a dragon's in the chill November air.

In the heat of the moment she had done exactly what she needed to do, evacuating Vesta to the safety of the front garden and letting the local fire department do what they do best.

'Actually, don't thank me, thank that fireman,' said Nelly, sitting alongside him in her heat-resistant slippers. 'He's the one that

put you out.'

The fireman and the fire engine had long gone. Their fire hose had been rolled up and returned to its spool after proving more than up to the job. Nelly could be grateful for small mercies. Although the lounge had been burnt to a cinder, the house was thankfully intact.

Still a little damp around the edges, Vesta's orange head was now thankfully flame-free and smoke-free too. To Nelly's relief, it also showed no signs of previous combustion either.

'Can we play that game again, Nelly?' Vesta honked.

'I think not,' sighed Nelly. 'I think the best thing we can do now is sit here quietly and wait for your Mumma and Dadda to come home.'

'OK,' honked Vesta, placing a consoling arm around Nelly's waist. 'I'm sure they won't mind. It was only a few flames.'

Nelly turned her head and raised both eyebrows to the heavens.

'A few flames?' she gasped. 'If the lounge hadn't had such good fire doors the whole house would have gone up!'

'Up where?' honked Vesta.

'Up in flames!' shuddered Nelly. 'That's where!'

'Are you sure we can't play that game again, Nelly, I was ever so good at it,' honked Vesta.

But Nelly wasn't listening. 'What do you think your Mumma and Dadda are going to say when they get home?' she murmured.

'About the game?' asked Vesta.

'No, about their lounge!' said Nelly. 'Honestly, Vesta, you don't seem the slightest bit concerned about the fire!'

'They'll probably say we need another air freshener,' he honked, 'but it's OK because we've got lots of spare ones in the loft.'

Nelly raised her bottom from the doorstep and paced to the end of the beech hedge. She could get a much better view of Truffle Lane from there.

She had decided not to talk about the fire to Vesta any more and instead rehearse her apology to May and Bryant.

She didn't have long to rehearse.

'Nelly! Vesta! look what we've found!' honked Bryant's voice excitedly.

Nelly looked down the driveway and

stared. Bryant and May were carrying the incinerated remains of an old sofa. It had been burnt beyond redemption and was nothing more than a soot-encrusted iron frame with blackened springs.

'The park keeper let us have it for NOTHING!' honked Bryant.

Nelly looked at her watch. It was four-thirty precisely.

'We found it in the park, Nelly,' honked May. 'Right in the middle of where that bonfire had been!'

'Isn't it beautiful!' honked Bryant.

'Isn't it marvellous!' honked May.

'PLUS!' honked May. 'There were two wonderfully blackened armchairs on the bonfire too!'

'We're going to have those delivered,' honked May.

Nelly stood agog as the two jubilant Hott Hed parents struggled up the driveway towards her with their prized possession.

'Doesn't it look comfortable, Nelly?' honked May, lowering her end of the sofa on to the driveway and then running her tong-like fingers across the charred remains of one arm.

'We know exactly where this is going!' honked May. 'But first we're going to have to change the colour of the lounge from red to completely black.'

'Yes,' honked May. 'A blackened three-piece suite in the middle of a red lounge wouldn't be matching at all.'

'We're Hott Heds, Nelly,' honked Bryant. 'Everything has to be matching!'

Nelly forced a smile and then cleared her throat with a dry rasp.

'Er, I might have been able to help you with that,' she mumbled, pushing the front door open with the flats of her palms. 'Vesta's *who fever* got a little bit out of control.'

'Have you been doing some cookery while we've been away, Nelly?'

'Kind of, but not exactly,' murmured Nelly, leading them down the hallway towards the lounge.

She had decided to let the room do the rest
of the talking.

'We can move the sofa
straight in!' honked Bryant,
jumping for joy.

The Hott Heds' beautiful red lounge was now as black as a witch's hat.

The red carpet was a carpet of black ash, the red walls were scorched blacker than burnt toast, the red picture frames had turned to charcoal, the red air freshener had melted and scorched into puddle of black treacle and the circular bench – well, that now had the sofa appeal of a giant incinerated doughnut.

Even the red fire buckets were black.

Bryant and May ambled affably into the hallway and sniffed deeply.

'That isn't Timber Inferno,' honked Bryant. 'Did you make the fragrance yourself?'

'Kind of,' said Nelly.

May was beside herself with excitement too.

'It's exactly the shade of blacky black black we were thinking of going for, Nelly,' she honked. 'What a clever monster sitter you are!'

Vesta looked at Nelly and slipped his hand into hers. 'I told you they wouldn't mind,' he honked.

'Are you sure you like it, May?' Nelly muttered, a little humbled. 'You don't think it looks a bit … burnt?'

'I'll tell you what I particularly like about what you've done, Nelly,' said May with a honk honk. 'It's the way you've brought the look and feel of the garden into the lounge!'

Nelly began to relax for the first time in quite a long time, but then jumped at the sound of an even louder HONK HONK! 'Goodness gracious,' honked May, 'who's that?'

'It's my dad,' Nelly replied, with a glance at
the front window.

'WHO?' honked Vesta, bursting into flames.

'Byeeeeeeeeee!' hollered Nelly.

TO THE GREENWOODS
AT NUMBER 74

HODDER CHILDREN'S BOOKS

First published in Great Britain in 2019 by Hodder and Stoughton

13 5 7 9 10 8 6 4 2

Text copyright © Kes Gray, 2019
Illustrations copyright © Chris Jevons, 2019

The moral rights of the author and illustrator have been asserted.

A CIP catalogue record for this book
is available from the British Library.

ISBN 978 1 444 94443 3

Printed and bound in great Britain by Clays Ltd, Elcograf S.p.A.

The paper and board used in this book
are made from wood from responsible sources.

MIX
Paper from
responsible sources
FSC® C104740

Hodder Children's Books
An imprint of
Hachette Children's Group
Part of Hodder and Stoughton
Carmelite House
50 Victoria Embankment
London EC4Y 0DZ

An Hachette UK Company
www.hachette.co.uk

www.hachettechildrens.co.uk